The Tracy Beaker Journal

Illustrated by Nick Sharratt

Written by Jacqueline Wilson

DOUBLEDAY

Welcome to my top secret, totally cool, completely brilliant journal! I'm Tracy Beaker. Mark the name, I'll be famous one day. But then, you already know that. You probably also know that I am

The Great Inventor of Extremely Outrageous Dares

Successful Writer

Star Football Player

Future Glamorous Hollywood Actress

Although this journal is all about ME, Tracy Beaker Superstar, I've generously allowed you some space to write down your own thoughts, ideas and dreams. I've always wanted to be reunited with my real mum, and I want to know all about YOUR family — how many brothers and sisters you've got, what you do on a typical weekend, and what annoying things your parents say to you and make you do. The grown-ups I'm unfortunate enough to know, Elaine the Pain for example, only seem to tell you what to do, go on and on about themselves, ask endless stupid questions and make personal comments. Useless.

I hope you have fun filling in this special secret Journal. And remember: when in doubt, go for it!

Tracy xxxxxxx

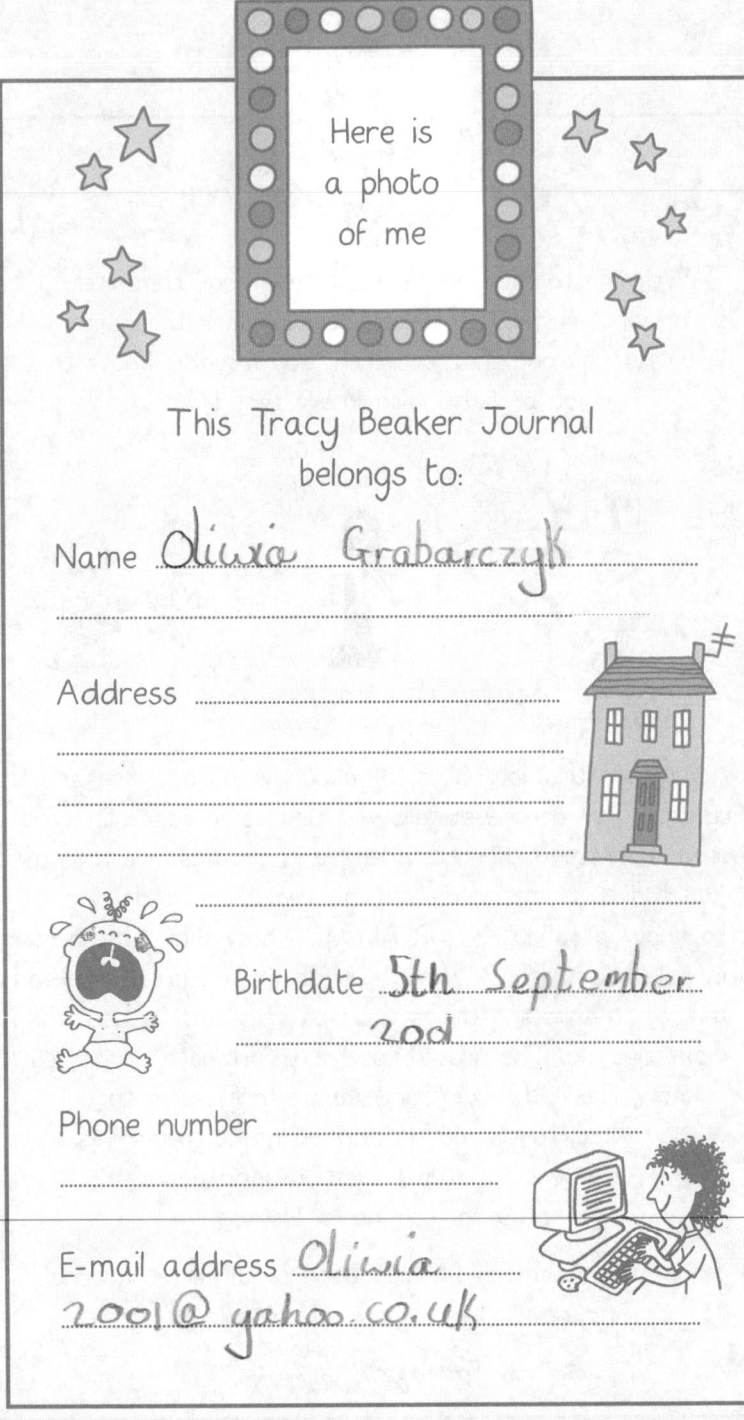

Here is
a photo
of me

This Tracy Beaker Journal
belongs to:

Name Olivia Grabarczyk

Address

Birthdate 5th September
2od

Phone number

E-mail address Olivia
2001@ yahoo.co.uk

My Family Album

Stick photos of your family members here,
preferably pulling the silliest faces possible!
Add photos of your friends too, if there's room.

Grandma

Dad

Grandad

Friend

Mum

Friend

Brother

Sister

Tracy Beaker Quiz

A QUIZ — all about ME!

Everyone knows that I'm bubbling over with natural charm, but only my biggest fans will be able to answer these tricky teasers...

 **1** What is my nickname for the children's home I live in? The ✓ dumbinground

 **2** What is the surname of my arch enemy, Justine? Littlewood

 **3** Which of these would I definitely NOT want to eat - YUK!

× Big Mac
× Popcorn
× Tapioca milk pudding ✗   ✓

What is the name of my art and drama teacher at Kinglea Junior School? _Miss spinkins_

✓

What did I pretend my real mum was for ages and ages?

× a dinner lady
× a movie star ✓
× a librarian

✓

What part do I play (completely brilliantly of course) in A CHRISTMAS CAROL?

Skonge

✓

What first name do I give horrible Mrs. V Bagley? Hee hee! ....

vomit

✓

Answers at the back

Tracy Beaker Wordsearch

See if you can be as clever as me and find some of my favourite things in this fiendishly hard puzzle!

POPCORN
FRENCH FRIES
BIG MAC
CAM
MAKE UP

MUM
HORROR FILMS
DISNEYLAND
WRITING STORIES
STRAWBERRY MILKSHAKE

Yuk! Crummy Boring Dull

```
S Q A B P O P C O R N W L H S D O M F W
R T O M W H G I K J P E Z O F A L B E Z
W I R A S C L W P R V X H R O P D J I S
Z L P A H R X Z F L W R X R C W I Z C E
S C W D W U I H J X S P U O P I S R O I
F E J B X B L S W E U A I R X L N W V R
A S K R H Z E X I R D W U F O J E G R O
P F W X E K P R S E F A Z I S H Y O S T
V R O D I J F U R R L P B L H W L V I S
I J L O A H X C E Y Q G U M Z S A A W G
H G W U C I V P J D M J F S R E N C J N
J L R N A X I L F E Z I P Z K W D X I I
S I E P F R H U A X D W L I V J L A E T
P R U E S Z D W E S H G U K E B S H D I
F P B I G M A C P U X V I P S X C G W R
E W V A W U K R I D L E Z U R H P D I W
B Z X D F L B W S G X A U O V X A A Z O
H C K I O M P C E I U C A M I R J K U A
W J L R X U S W A H Z X J G K W K P E I
P U E K A M R O Z P D E T Q E A I W F R
```

Answers at the back

All About Me

And don't forget ME!

What three words best describe you?

I think friendly,
tasnebol and
staring!!

TRACY

Elaine the Pain says I am 'lively and chatty' but what she really means is 'cheeky, difficult and bossy'.

Your favourite food

cheolate cack
and eggyed (its
my own creasion)

TRACY

Mine is birthday cake! Or maybe Smarties. Or Big Mac and french fries. Or maybe Mike's spaghetti bolognaise. Or...

Your favourite colour

blue white and
purple

TRACY

A gruesome blood-red!

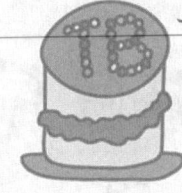

Your favourite book

starring tray beaker of corse!

TRACY
Cam gave me loads of brilliant books for Christmas, I can't pick just one. Have YOU read any of these?

Your favourite films

all srek films and family and twiligth

TRACY
All of the films my mum has starred in, plus scary horror films. Oh, and The Wizard of Oz.

Your favourite animals

dog, espesrally tala hamsters

TRACY
Mine are dogs. Especially Rottweilers. So all my enemies had better WATCH OUT!

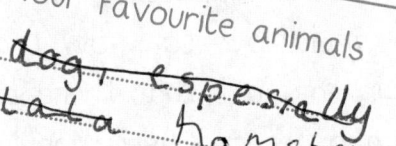

Your favourite activities

cretive games. I like making stuff but i hate sowing!

TRACY
Does playing with make-up count? Also the Dare Game, of which I am the undisputed champion, of course.

Jacqueline Wilson on Tracy Beaker

Tracy Beaker is by far the most popular of all the characters I've ever invented. How she would love to know that! She would just glory in the fact that there are now three books about her, a very popular long-running television series, a magazine, a musical, and all sorts of merchandising, from pyjamas to pencil cases!

I got the idea for *The Story of Tracy Beaker* from seeing photos of children in care in my local paper, all longing to be fostered. I looked at those touching pictures and wondered what it would be like to be advertised in that way. It would be great if you found brilliant foster parents as a result, but how would you feel in no one at all came forward to meet up with you?

I decided to write a story about a tough feisty little girl in a children's home who gets advertised like this.

I knew almost straight away that I was going to call her Tracy. It seemed a perfect modern street-wise bouncy sort of name. I had problems finding a suitable surname. I was thinking about it when I was lolling in my bath one morning. I peered all round the steamy room for some kind of inspiration. There aren't a lot of possibilities in the average bathroom! I wondered about Tracy Flannel, Tracy Soap, Tracy Tap, Tracy Toothbrush, Tracy Toilet — and decided I'd never ever find a sensible surname that way. I got on with washing my hair and then reached for the old plastic Snoopy beaker I kept on the side of the bath to rinse all the shampoo away. I stared at it. Tracy Beaker? Yes, I had the right name at last.

Jacqueline Wilson

My Favourite Hopes and Dreams

One day I will live in my very own house. It'll have a huge bedroom just for me with special bunk beds and a Mickey Mouse alarm clock.

I'm going to be a world-famous actress, wowing crowds with my star quality. Or I'm going to make my fortune as a writer, you wait and see.

My number one top dream this year is to swim with dolphins.

to become a
Dancer and singer
just like bella
throme did (shes
my idoll)

Elmo to be
allways alive, to live
with him foreva.

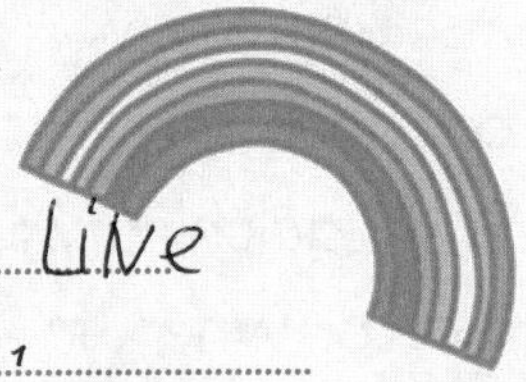

My Worst Worries and Problems

As you know, I'm totally fearless and don't ever cry, but my life can't be Big Macs and swimming with dolphins ALL the time. Always remember my motto: when in doubt, go for it!

....

....

....

....

....

....

....

....

....

....

....

....

....

....

1 JANUARY

Happy new year

2 JANUARY

3 JANUARY

4 JANUARY

School Today

5 JANUARY

6 JANUARY

7 JANUARY

8 JANUARY

9 JANUARY

10 JANUARY

11 JANUARY

12 JANUARY

13 JANUARY

14 JANUARY

15 JANUARY

16 JANUARY

17 JANUARY

18 JANUARY

19 JANUARY

20 JANUARY

21 JANUARY

22 JANUARY

23 JANUARY

24 JANUARY

25 JANUARY

26 JANUARY

27 JANUARY

28 JANUARY

29 JANUARY

30 JANUARY

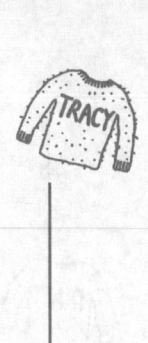

31 JANUARY

1 FEBRUARY

2 FEBRUARY

3 FEBRUARY

4 FEBRUARY

5 FEBRUARY

6 FEBRUARY

7 FEBRUARY

8 FEBRUARY

9 FEBRUARY

10 FEBRUARY

11 FEBRUARY

12 FEBRUARY

13 FEBRUARY

14 FEBRUARY

Valentine's Day

15 FEBRUARY

16 FEBRUARY

17 FEBRUARY

18 FEBRUARY

19 FEBRUARY

20 FEBRUARY

21 FEBRUARY

22 FEBRUARY

23 FEBRUARY

24 FEBRUARY

25 FEBRUARY

26 FEBRUARY

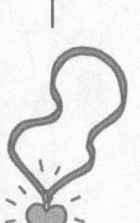

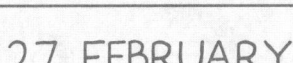

27 FEBRUARY

28 FEBRUARY

29 FEBRUARY

Leap year only

1 MARCH

2 MARCH

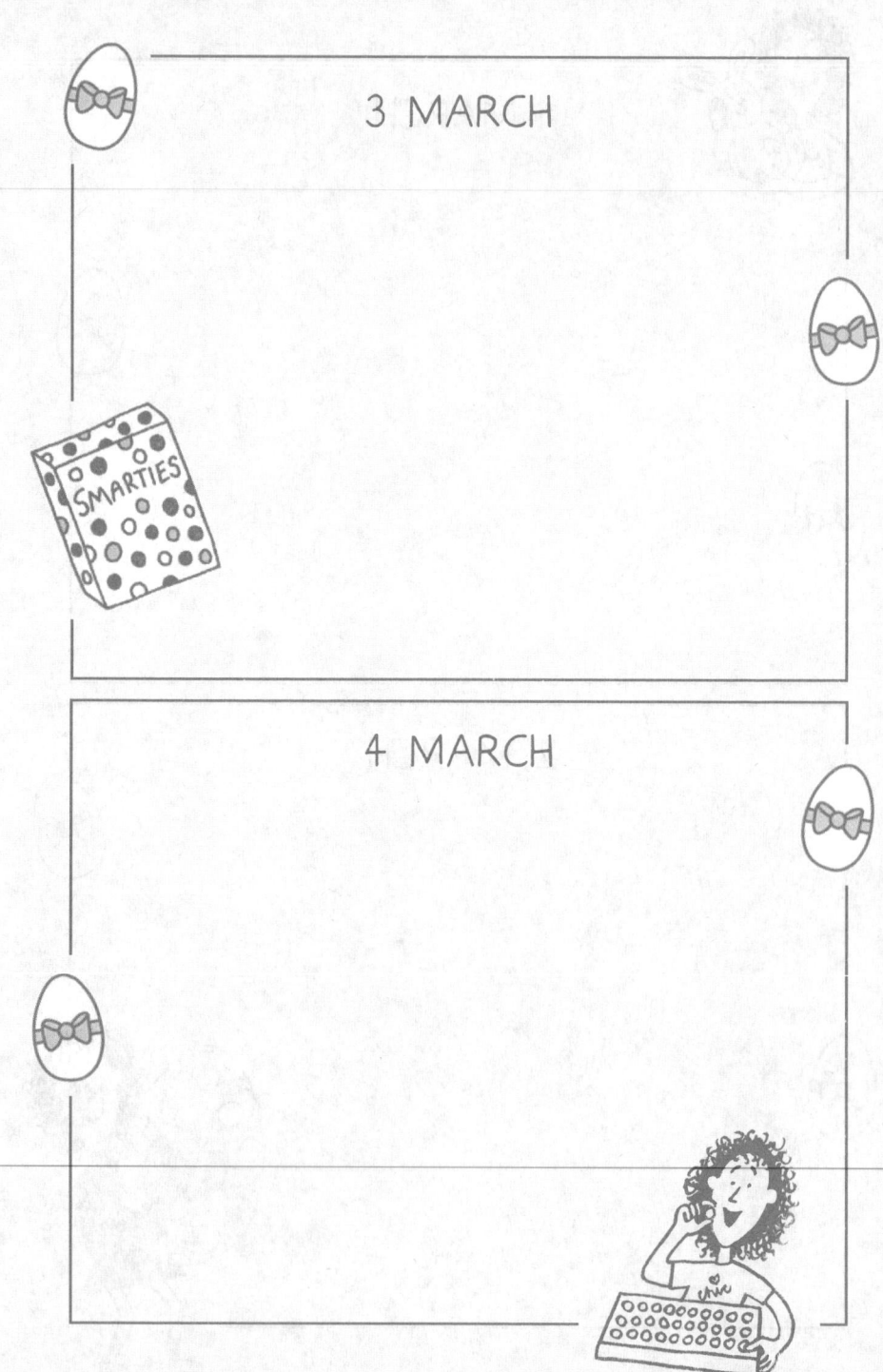

3 MARCH

4 MARCH

5 MARCH

6 MARCH

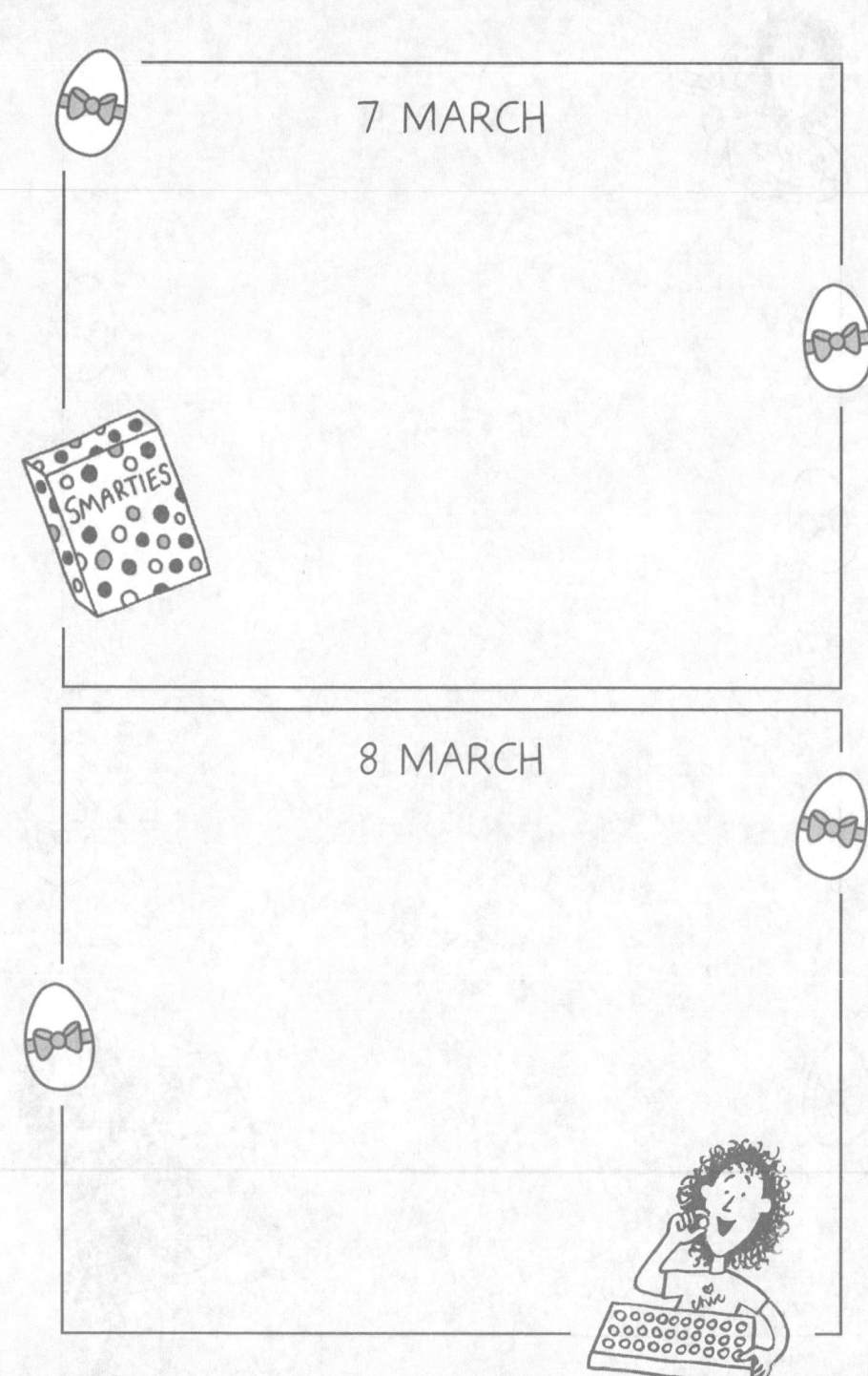

7 MARCH

8 MARCH

9 MARCH

10 MARCH

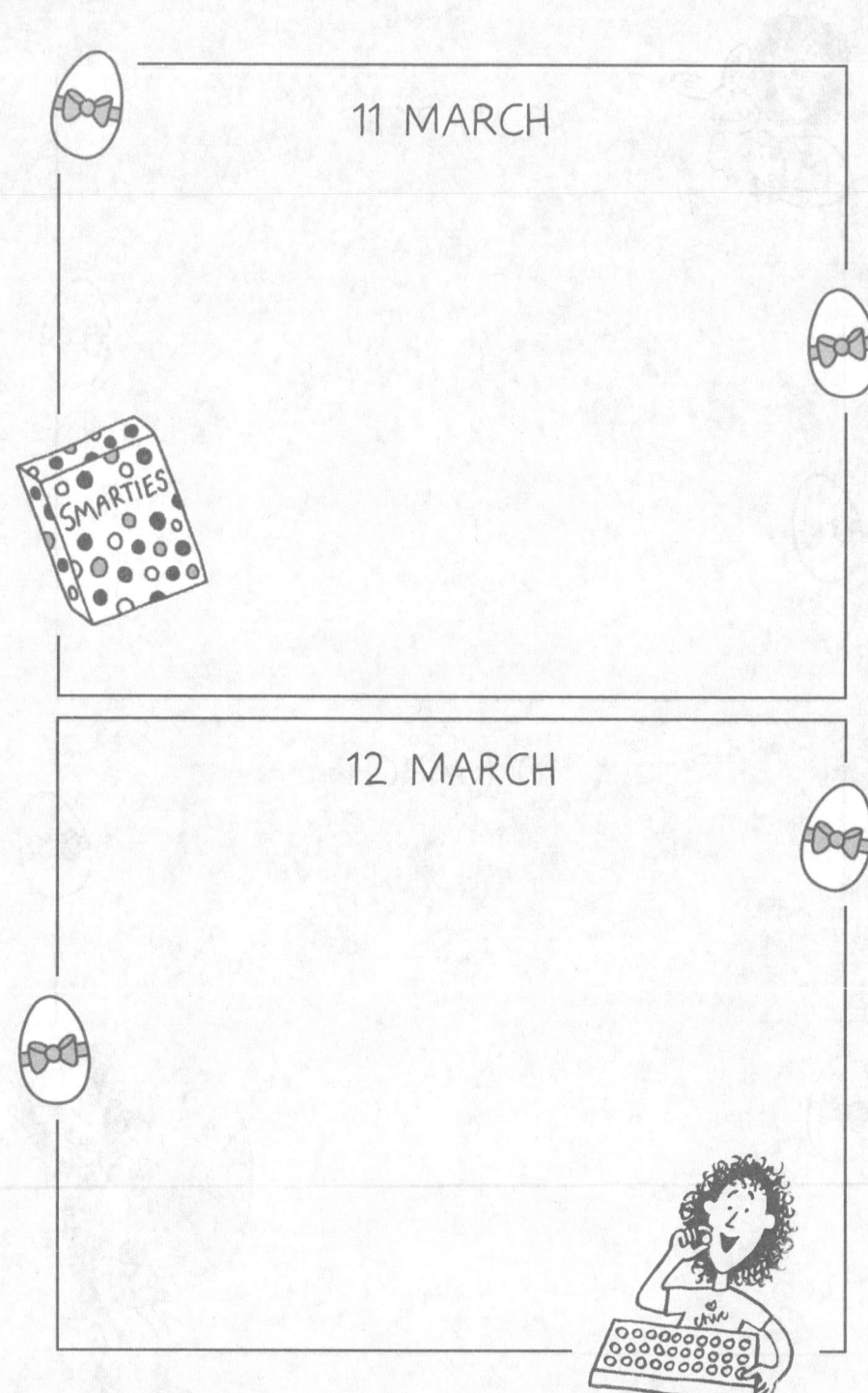

11 MARCH

12 MARCH

13 MARCH

14 MARCH

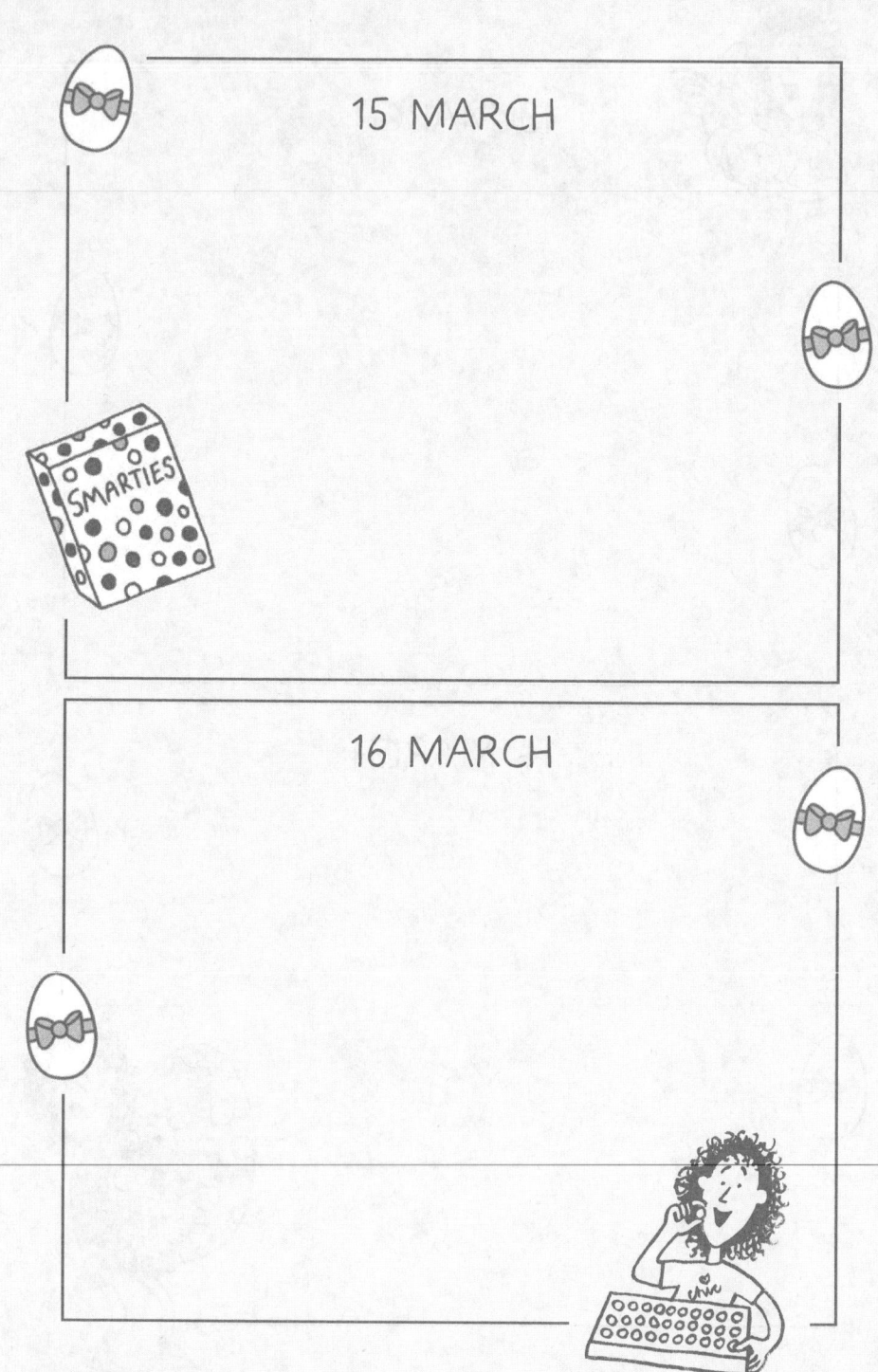

15 MARCH

16 MARCH

17 MARCH

18 MARCH

19 MARCH

20 MARCH

21 MARCH

22 MARCH

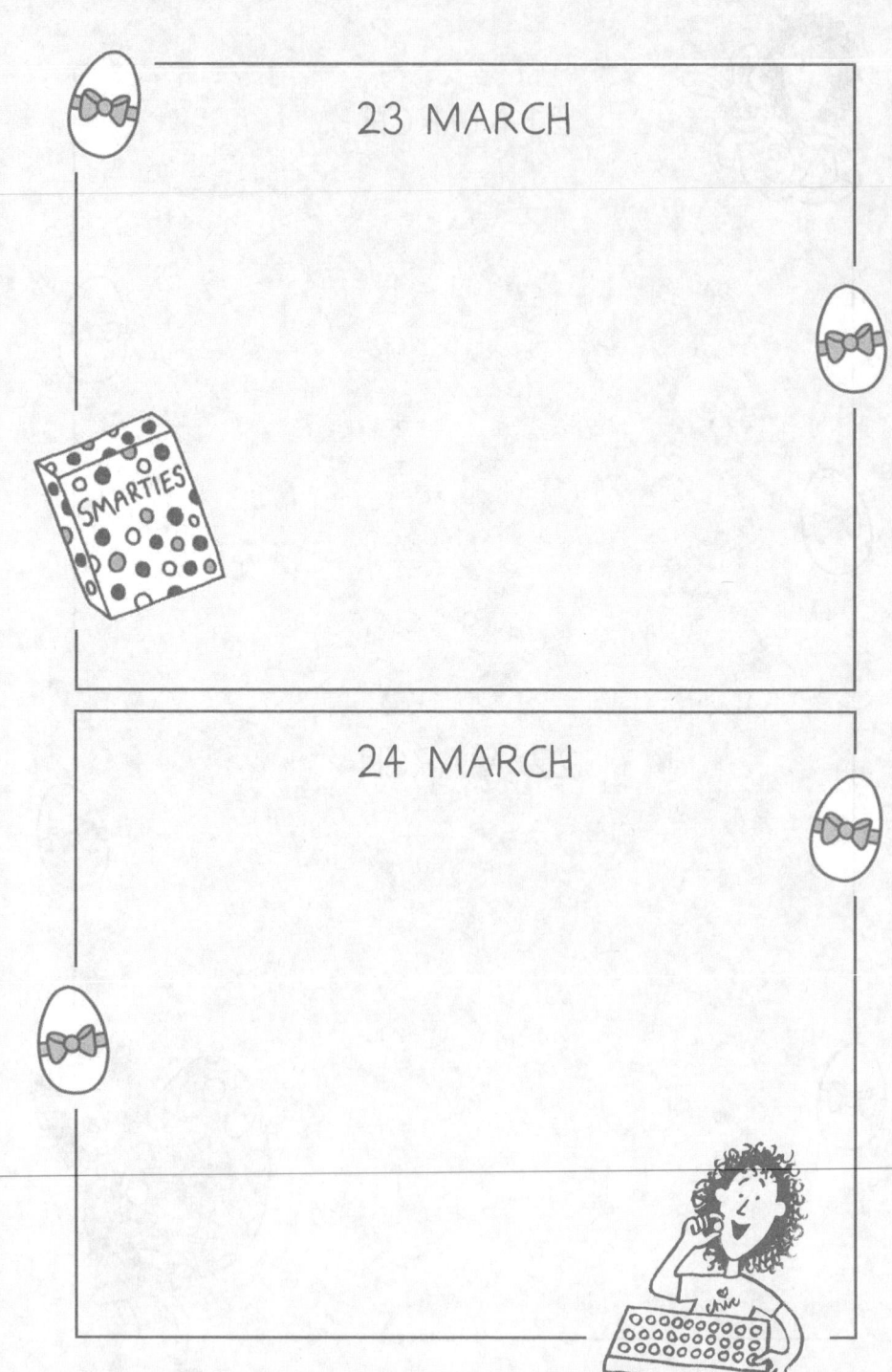

23 MARCH

24 MARCH

25 MARCH

26 MARCH

27 MARCH

28 MARCH

29 MARCH

30 MARCH

31 MARCH

1 APRIL

2 APRIL

3 APRIL

4 APRIL

5 APRIL

6 APRIL

7 APRIL

8 APRIL

9 APRIL

10 APRIL

11 APRIL

12 APRIL

13 APRIL

14 APRIL

15 APRIL

16 APRIL

17 APRIL

18 APRIL

19 APRIL

20 APRIL

21 APRIL

22 APRIL

23 APRIL

24 APRIL

25 APRIL

26 APRIL

27 APRIL

28 APRIL

29 APRIL

30 APRIL

1 MAY

2 MAY

3 MAY

4 MAY

5 MAY

6 MAY

7 MAY

8 MAY

birthday cake
yum!

MY BIRTHDAY!
And Weedy Peter's too, but mine is
more important, obviously.

9 MAY

10 MAY

11 MAY

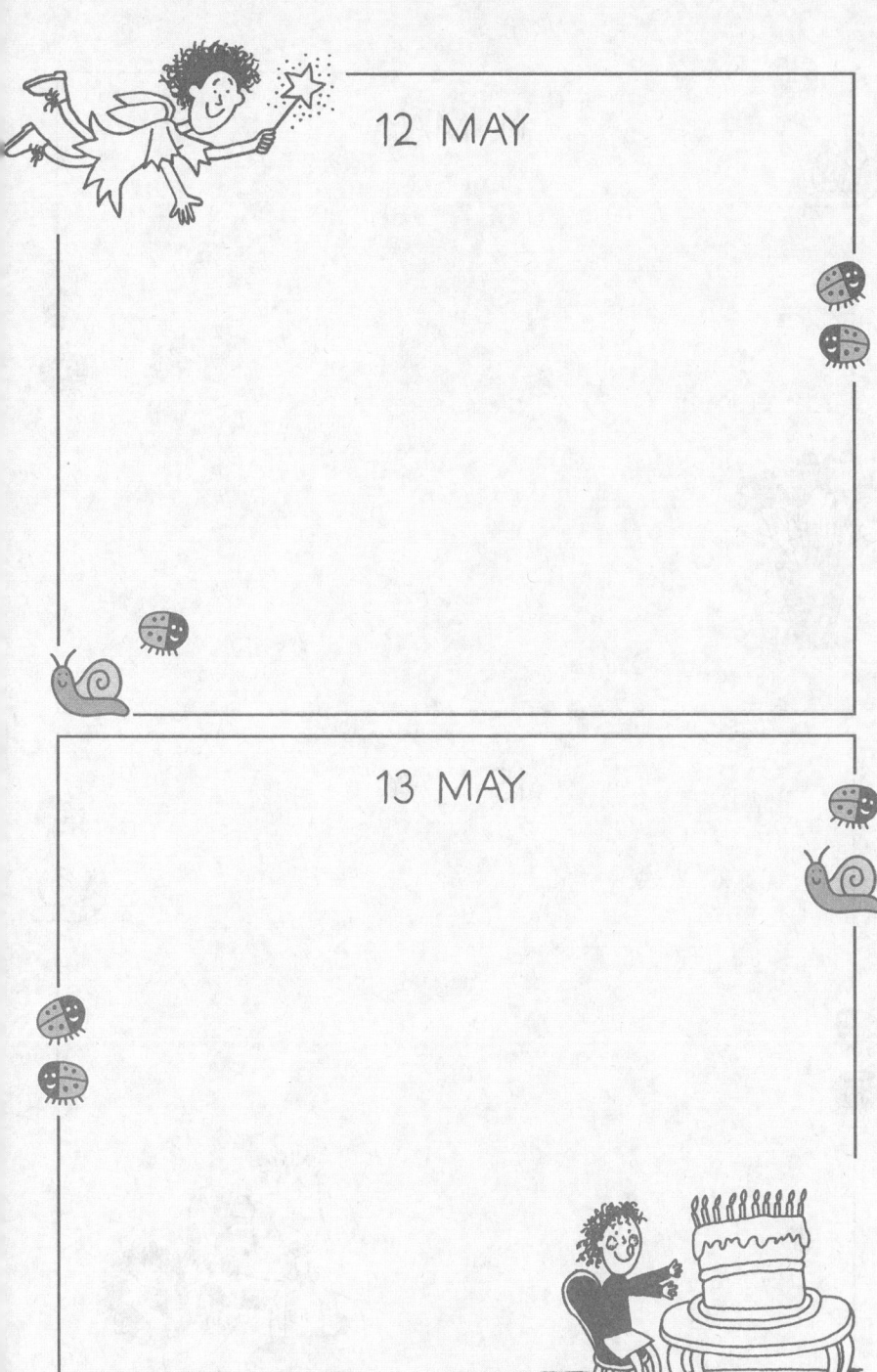

12 MAY

13 MAY

14 MAY

15 MAY

16 MAY

17 MAY

18 MAY

19 MAY

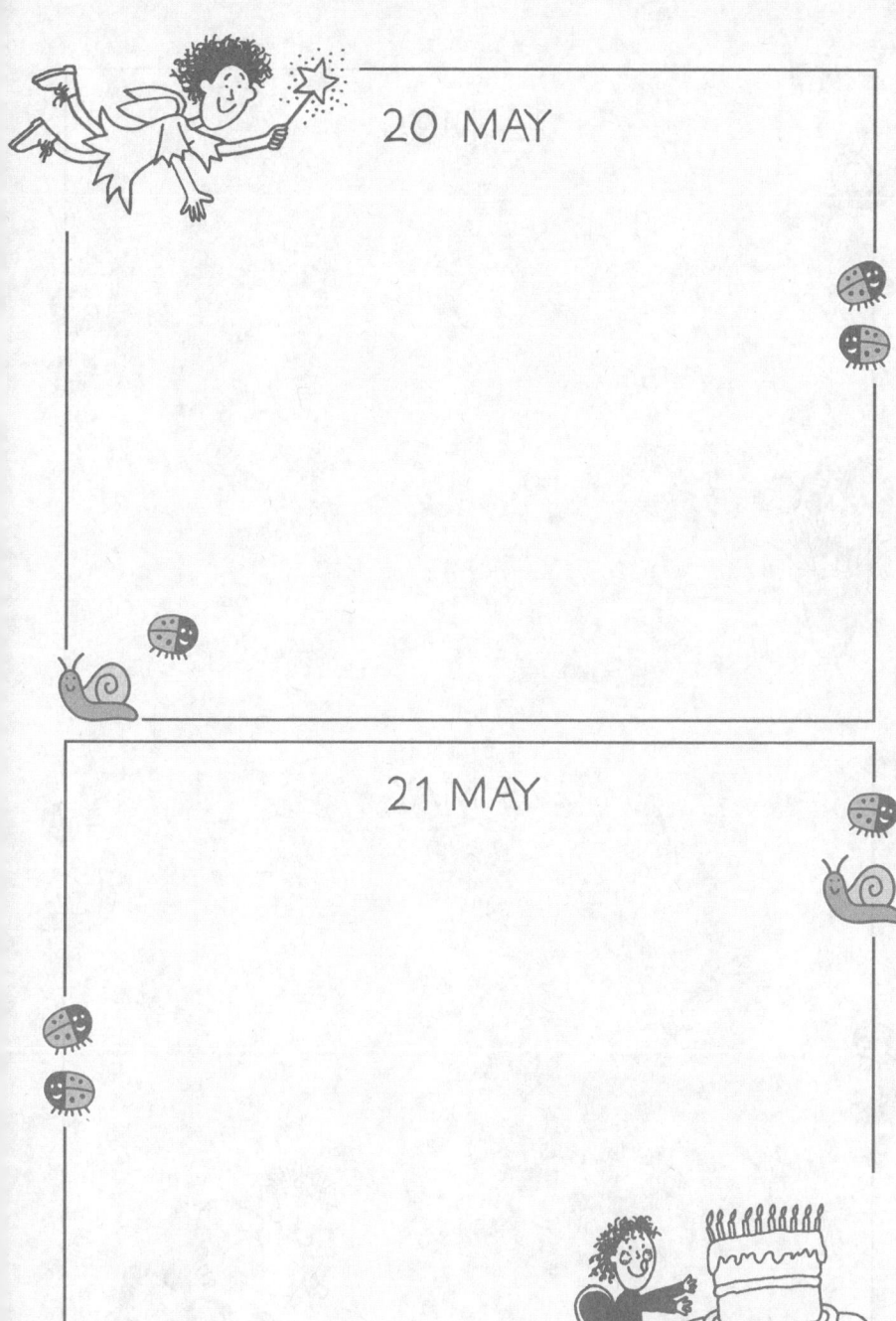

20 MAY

21 MAY

22 MAY

23 MAY

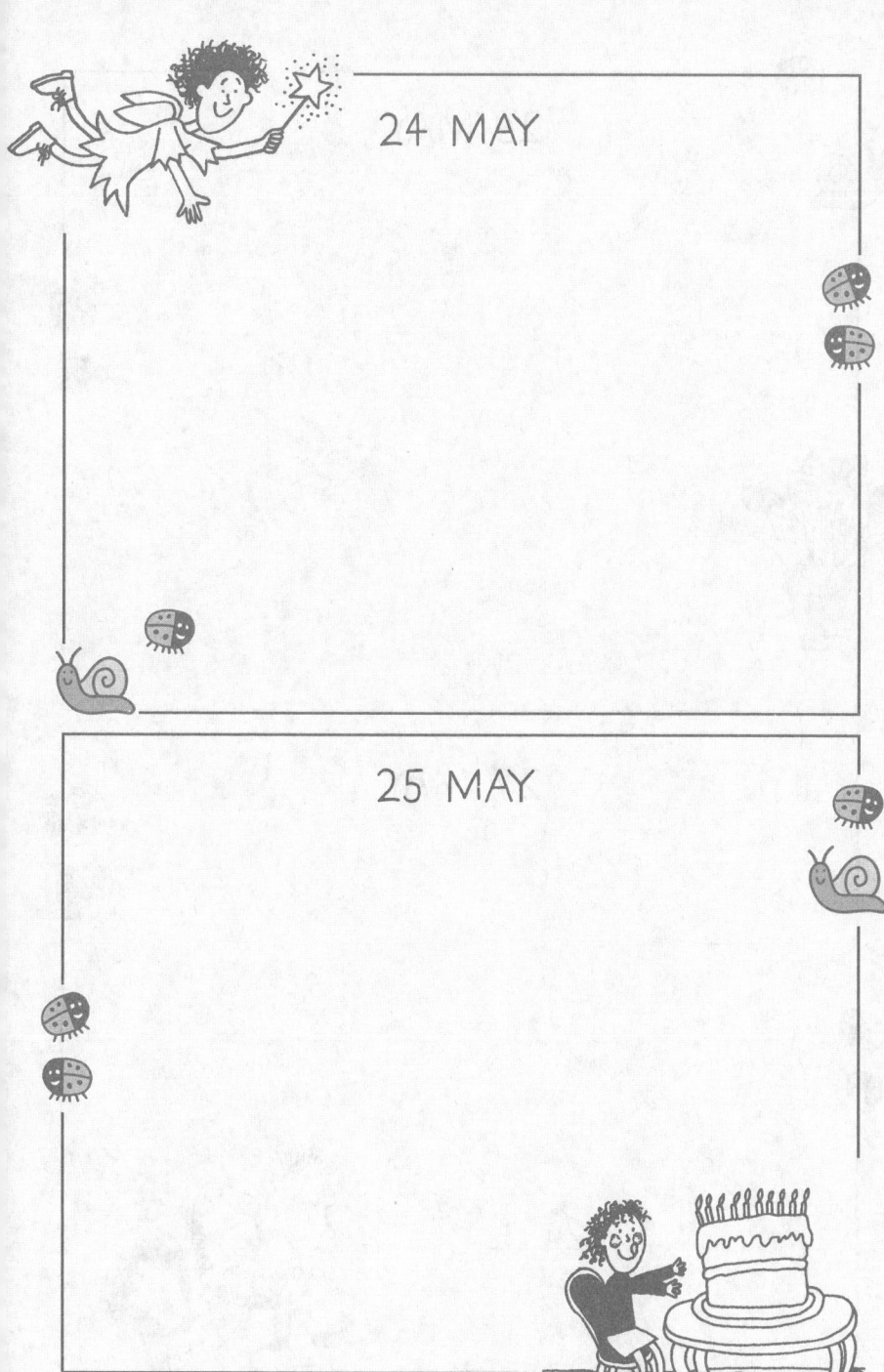

24 MAY

25 MAY

26 MAY

27 MAY

28 MAY

29 MAY

30 MAY

31 MAY

1 JUNE

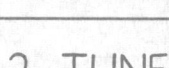

2 JUNE

3 JUNE

4 JUNE

5 JUNE

6 JUNE

7 JUNE

8 JUNE

9 JUNE

10 JUNE

11 JUNE

12 JUNE

13 JUNE

14 JUNE

15 JUNE

16 JUNE

17 JUNE

18 JUNE

19 JUNE

20 JUNE

21 JUNE

22 JUNE

23 JUNE

24 JUNE

25 JUNE

26 JUNE

27 JUNE

28 JUNE

29 JUNE

30 JUNE

1 JULY

2 JULY

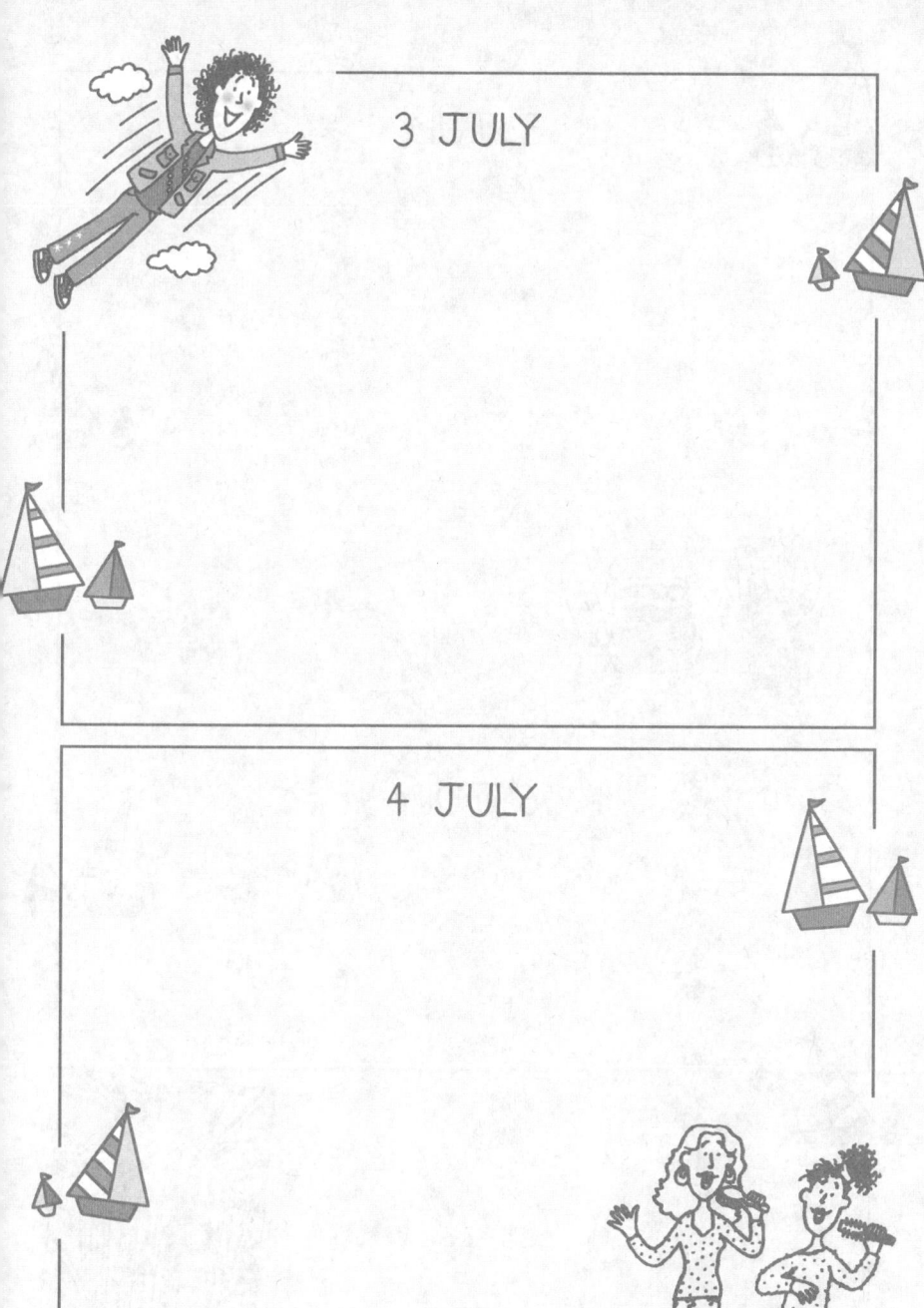

3 JULY

4 JULY

5 JULY

6 JULY

7 JULY

8 JULY

9 JULY

10 JULY

11 JULY

12 JULY

13 JULY

14 JULY

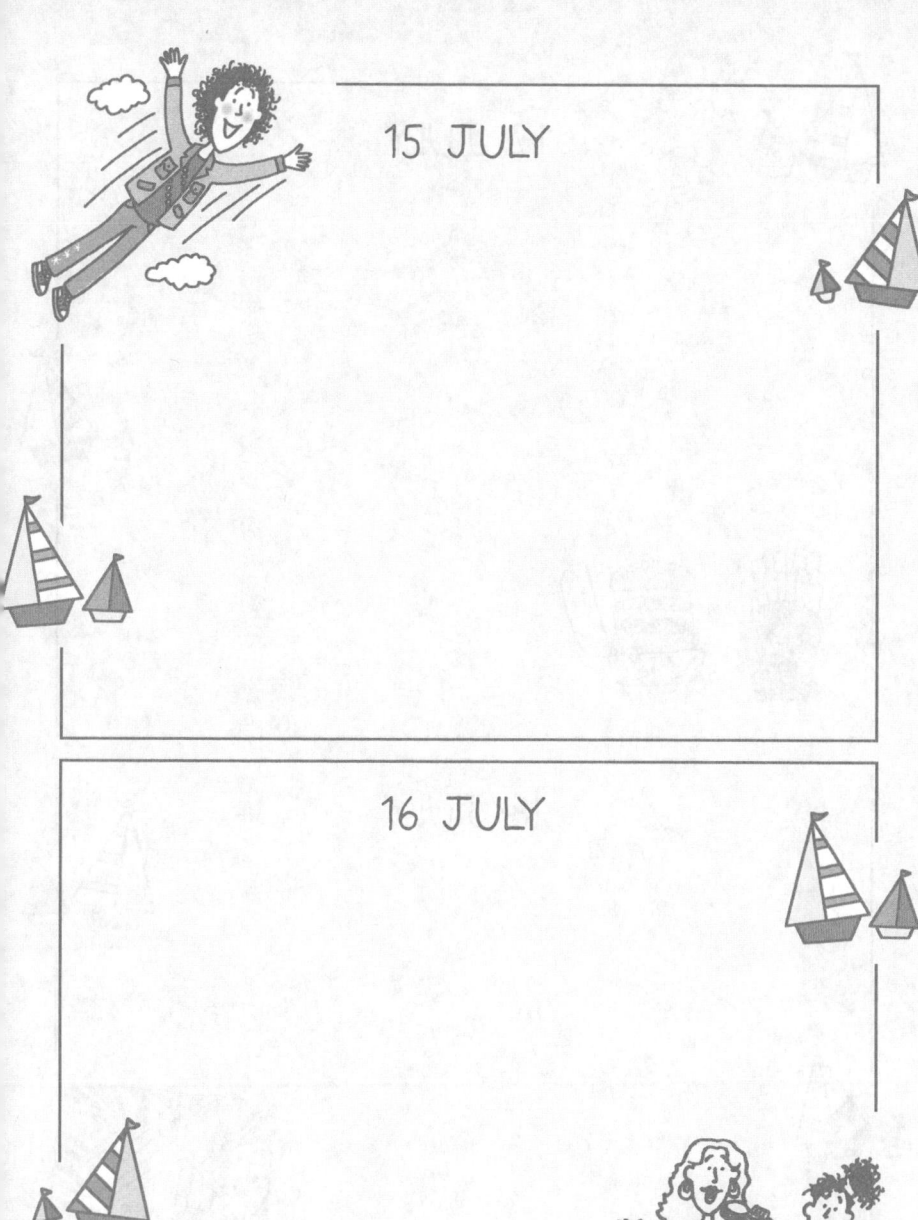

15 JULY

16 JULY

17 JULY

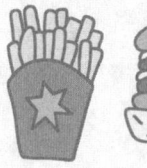 

18 JULY

19 JULY

20 JULY

21 JULY

22 JULY

23 JULY

24 JULY

25 JULY

26 JULY

27 JULY

28 JULY

29 JULY

30 JULY

31 JULY

1 AUGUST

2 AUGUST

3 AUGUST

4 AUGUST

5 AUGUST

6 AUGUST

7 AUGUST

8 AUGUST

9 AUGUST

10 AUGUST

11 AUGUST

12 AUGUST

13 AUGUST

14 AUGUST

15 AUGUST

16 AUGUST

17 AUGUST

18 AUGUST

19 AUGUST

20 AUGUST

21 AUGUST

22 AUGUST

23 AUGUST

24 AUGUST

25 AUGUST

26 AUGUST

27 AUGUST

28 AUGUST

29 AUGUST

30 AUGUST

31 AUGUST

1 SEPTEMBER

2 SEPTEMBER

3 SEPTEMBER

4 SEPTEMBER

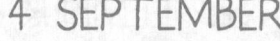

5 SEPTEMBER

My birthday!

11!

6 SEPTEMBER

7 SEPTEMBER

8 SEPTEMBER

9 SEPTEMBER

10 SEPTEMBER

11 SEPTEMBER

12 SEPTEMBER

13 SEPTEMBER

14 SEPTEMBER

15 SEPTEMBER

16 SEPTEMBER

17 SEPTEMBER

18 SEPTEMBER

19 SEPTEMBER

20 SEPTEMBER

21 SEPTEMBER

22 SEPTEMBER

23 SEPTEMBER

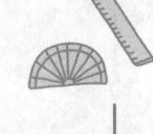

24 SEPTEMBER

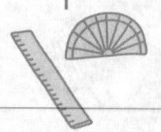

25 SEPTEMBER

26 SEPTEMBER

27 SEPTEMBER

28 SEPTEMBER

29 SEPTEMBER

30 SEPTEMBER

1 OCTOBER

2 OCTOBER

3 OCTOBER

4 OCTOBER

5 OCTOBER

6 OCTOBER

7 OCTOBER

8 OCTOBER

9 OCTOBER

10 OCTOBER

11 OCTOBER

12 OCTOBER

13 OCTOBER

14 OCTOBER

15 OCTOBER

16 OCTOBER

17 OCTOBER

18 OCTOBER

19 OCTOBER

20 OCTOBER

21 OCTOBER

22 OCTOBER

23 OCTOBER

24 OCTOBER

25 OCTOBER

26 OCTOBER

27 OCTOBER

28 OCTOBER

29 OCTOBER

30 OCTOBER

31 OCTOBER

1 NOVEMBER

2 NOVEMBER

3 NOVEMBER

4 NOVEMBER

5 NOVEMBER

Bonfire Night

6 NOVEMBER

7 NOVEMBER

8 NOVEMBER

9 NOVEMBER

10 NOVEMBER

11 NOVEMBER

12 NOVEMBER

13 NOVEMBER

14 NOVEMBER

15 NOVEMBER

16 NOVEMBER

17 NOVEMBER

18 NOVEMBER

19 NOVEMBER

20 NOVEMBER

21 NOVEMBER

22 NOVEMBER

23 NOVEMBER

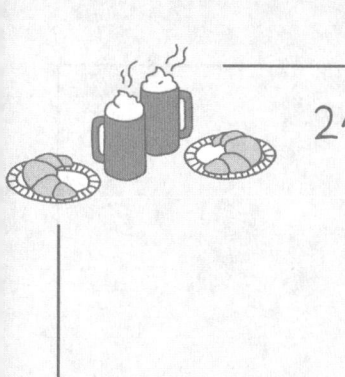

24 NOVEMBER

25 NOVEMBER

26 NOVEMBER

27 NOVEMBER

28 NOVEMBER

29 NOVEMBER

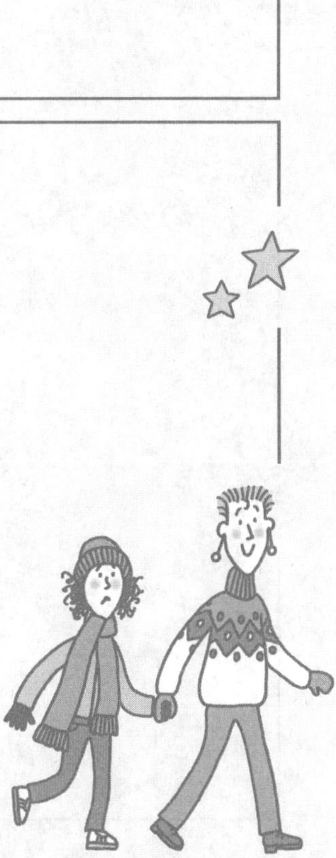

30 NOVEMBER

1 DECEMBER

EEYORE! EEYORE!

2 DECEMBER

3 DECEMBER

4 DECEMBER

5 DECEMBER

EEYORE! EEYORE!

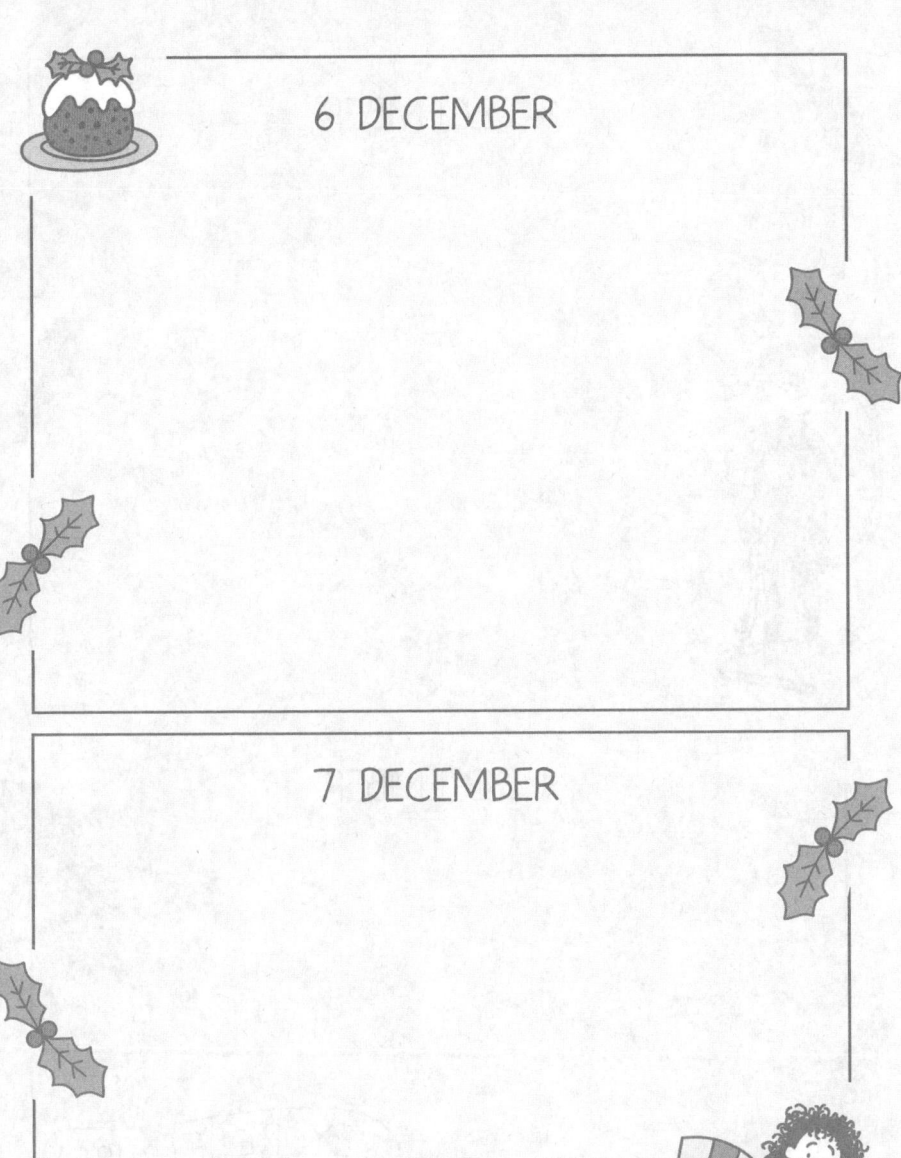

6 DECEMBER

7 DECEMBER

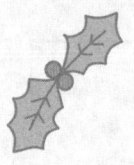

8 DECEMBER

9 DECEMBER

10 DECEMBER

11 DECEMBER

12 DECEMBER

13 DECEMBER

EEYORE! EEYORE!

14 DECEMBER

15 DECEMBER

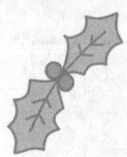

16 DECEMBER

17 DECEMBER

Jacqueline Wilson's Birthday

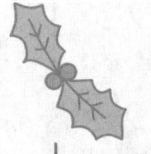

EEYORE! EEYORE!

18 DECEMBER

19 DECEMBER

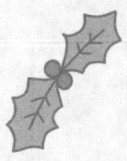

20 DECEMBER

My star turn in A CHRISTMAS CAROL!

21 DECEMBER

22 DECEMBER

23 DECEMBER

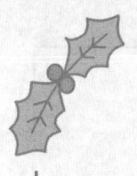

24   DECEMBER

25 DECEMBER

Christmas Day

EEYORE! EEYORE!

26 DECEMBER

Boxing Day

27 DECEMBER

28 DECEMBER

29 DECEMBER

EEYORE! EEYORE!

30 DECEMBER

31 DECEMBER

ANSWERS TO TRACY BEAKER QUIZ

1. The Dumping Ground
2. Littlewood
3. Tapioca milk pudding
4. Miss Simpkins
5. a movie star
6. Scrooge
7. Vomit

WORDSEARCH SOLUTION

How many did you find?

Join the FREE online

Jacqueline Wilson

★ FAN CLUB ★

Read Jacqueline's monthly diary, look up
tour info, receive fan club e-newsletters.

All this and more, including a fab
message board, members'
jokes and loads of exclusive top offers

Visit www.jacquelinewilson.co.uk
for more info!

Have you read all these Jacqueline Wilson books?

Also available by Jacqueline Wilson

Published in Corgi Pups,
for beginner readers:

THE DINOSAUR'S PACKED LUNCH
THE MONSTER STORY-TELLER

Published in Young Corgi,
for newly confident readers:

LIZZIE ZIPMOUTH
SLEEPOVERS

Published in Doubleday/Corgi Yearling Books:

BAD GIRLS
THE BED & BREAKFAST STAR
BEST FRIENDS
BURIED ALIVE!
CANDYFLOSS
THE CAT MUMMY
CLEAN BREAK
CLIFFHANGER
THE DARE GAME
DOUBLE ACT
GLUBBSLYME

THE ILLUSTRATED MUM
JACKY DAYDREAM
THE LOTTIE PROJECT
MIDNIGHT
THE MUM-MINDER
MY SISTER JODIE
SECRETS
STARRING TRACY BEAKER
THE STORY OF TRACY BEAKER
THE SUITCASE KID
VICKY ANGEL
THE WORRY WEBSITE

Available from Doubleday/Corgi Books,
for older readers:

THE DIAMOND GIRLS
DUSTBIN BABY
GIRLS IN LOVE
GIRLS OUT LATE
GIRLS UNDER PRESSURE
GIRLS IN TEARS
LOLA ROSE
LOVE LESSONS

Jacky Daydream

by Jacqueline Wilson

Everybody knows Tracy Beaker, Jacqueline Wilson's
best-loved character. But what do they know about the
little girl who grew up to become Jacqueline Wilson?

How she played with paper dolls like April
in *Dustbin Baby*.

How she dealt with an unpredictable father like
Prue in *Love Lessons*.

How she chose new toys in Hamleys like Dolphin
in *The Illustrated Mum*.

How she enjoyed Christmas like Em in *Clean Break*.

How she sat entrance exams like Ruby in *Double Act*.

But most of all how she loved reading and writing
stories. Losing herself in a new world was the best
possible way she could think of spending her time.
From the very first story she wrote, *Meet the Maggots*,
it was clear that this little girl had a very vivid
imagination. But who would've guessed that she would
grow up to be the mega-bestselling, award-winning
Jacqueline Wilson!

Starring Tracy Beaker

by Jacqueline Wilson

Tracy Beaker is back . . . and she's just
desperate for a role in her school play.
They're performing *A Christmas Carol* and for
one worrying moment, the irrepressible Tracy
thinks she might not even get to play one of
the unnamed street urchins. But then she
is cast in the main role. Can she manage to act
grumpy and difficult enough to play Scrooge?
Well, she does have a bit of help on that front
from Justine Pain-In-The-Bum Littlewood . . .

As Tracy prepares for her big moment,
Cam is the one helping her learn her lines.
But all Tracy wants to know is if her film-star
mum will come to watch her in her starring role.

'Exciting and thrilling, funny and
full of suspense' *First News*

THE TRACY BEAKER JOURNAL
A DOUBLEDAY BOOK
978 0 385 61543 3

Published in Great Britain by Doubleday Books,
an imprint of Random House Children's Books

This edition published 2008

1 3 5 7 9 10 8 6 4 2

Text copyright © Jacqueline Wilson, 1991, 1992, 1993, 1994, 1995, 1996,
1997, 1998, 1999, 2000, 2001, 2002, 2003, 2004, 2005, 2006, 2007, 2008
Illustrations copyright © Nick Sharratt, 1991, 1992, 1993, 1994, 1995, 1996,
1997, 1998, 1999, 2000, 2001, 2002, 2003, 2004, 2005, 2006, 2007, 2008

The right of Jacqueline Wilson to be identified as the author of this work
has been asserted in accordance with the Copyright, Designs and Patents Act 1988.

Compiled by Lauren Buckland

The Random House Group Limited makes every effort to ensure that the papers
used in its books are made from trees that have been legally sourced from
well-managed and credibly certified forests. Our paper procurement policy can
be found at: www.randomhouse.co.uk/paper.htm

RANDOM HOUSE CHILDREN'S BOOKS
61-63 Uxbridge Road, London W5 5SA

www.kidsatrandomhouse.co.uk

Addresses for companies within The Random House Group Limited
can be found at: www.randomhouse.co.uk/offices.htm

THE RANDOM HOUSE GROUP Limited Reg. No. 954009

A CIP catalogue record for this book is available from the British Library.

Printed and bound in China